CLOSE TO SPIDER MAN

CLOSE
TO
SPIDER MAN

†

stories

Ivan E. Coyote

ARSENAL PULP PRESS
Vancouver

CLOSE TO SPIDER MAN
Copyright © 2000 by Ivan E. Coyote

Third printing: 2011

ARSENAL PULP PRESS
211 East Georgia St, Suite 101
Vancouver, BC
Canada V6A 1Z6
arsenalpulp.com

The publisher gratefully acknowledges the support of the Canada Council
for the Arts and the British Columbia Arts Council for its publishing
program, and the Government of Canada through the Canada Book
Fund for its publishing activities.

This is a work of fiction. Any resemblance of characters to persons,
living or dead, is purely coincidental.

Earlier versions of "She Comes Home a Moth" and
"You're not in Kansas Anymore" appeared in *The Loop*,
and versions of "Walks Like," "Three Left Turns," and "Manifestation"
appeared in *Boys Like Her* by Taste This (Press Gang, 1999).

Designed by Solo

Printed and bound in Canada

Canadian Cataloguing in Publication Data:
Coyote, Ivan E. (Ivan Elizabeth), 1969-
Close to Spider Man

ISBN 978-1-55152-086-5

I. Title.
PS8555.O99C56 2000   C813'.6   C00-910925-0
PR9199.3.C6682C56 2000

This book is dedicated to Joe Hiscott, my un-partner, and to Pat Daws, my mother, for letting me tell it my way.

ACKNOWLEDGMENTS
I would like to thank Zoë Eakle, Anna Camilleri,
and Lyndell Montgomery, my fellow authors of
Boys Like Her and stagemates, for their friendship and
talent. They have, and continue to be, a source of inspiration
and/or butt-kicks, whichever is deemed to be most necessary
at the time. Thanks also to my cousin Trish Leeper, fellow
artist in the family, for her belief in me and for explaining
to our relatives that I do indeed have a real job. Love and
thanks to Chantal Sundquist and Tamara Brewster
for being the best brothers a fella could ask for.

Many thanks to Brian Lam and Blaine Kyllo
and the folks at Arsenal Pulp Press for keeping
it all together, even when I ran off with the circus.

CLOSE TO SPIDER MAN

SHE COMES HOME A MOTH

EVERYONE ON OUR STREET HAD KIDS.
It was that kind of street: Hemlock Street, a dusty little L-
shaped road with a fence at one end. I wouldn't call the place
where our street stopped a dead end, though, because that's
where it all started: the old dump road, the power line, the veins
in a leaf-like network of trails that led to our places. The places
we built forts, tobogganed in green garbage bags, and learned
how to ride after our dads took the blocks off our pedals.

My mom tells the story of how she met your mom, awake
in the night, pacing in front of the living room window, a
small, crying bundle in her arms. That bundle was me. There
was only one other light on the block, in the house right across
the street. Inside the light stood a woman, holding a baby. She
shrugged, a you-too, huh? kind of movement with her shoulders, and waved at my mother.

They didn't get a chance to meet for a couple more days —
your mom worked in the evenings and mine in the day — but
they would be together late at night, in their windows, with

the road and the dark between them, in separate circles of light.

One Friday night your mom knocked on our door. "Could you take her?" She meant you. "Pierre and I, we need to go away for a couple of hours. Can you watch my baby? Her name is Valerie."

So I only remember a time when there was you. You can remember details, whole conversations and dates; I cannot. I remember colours, our hands stained with cranberries. You had long brown hair. We both had a pair of red pants.

We were always together. Your dad called us cheese and crackers. We never kissed.

I liked how you hardly said anything when there were adults around, but how when we were alone your soft voice spilled out plans: now how 'bout we play this? We usually fundamentally disagreed on what we were or should be playing, but never considered other partners.

I remember when your grandmother came to visit from France; her voice was bigger than she was, and your father was the interpreter. She shook her head and laughed at my mother. "How come everyday you send this one out looking like a butterfly, and she comes home a moth?"

You always kept your knees clean.

My mom let us use her bike one day. We were going to the store, and her bike had a basket in front. It was way too big for me, but I pedalled with much concentration, my tongue pressed between my lips. You sat on the seat, legs dangling, your summer-brown thumbs in my belt loops.

We had to go down the big hill next to the meadow where boys smoked cigarettes sometimes, and your grip on my waist tightened. "You're driving too *faaaast*. Slow *dooown*." Your voice was bumpy from the gravel and potholes on the road.

Unfamiliar with the physics of a three-speed, I slammed on what turned out to be the front brakes, and that's when the tragedy happened. The road rash would heal, the hole in the knee of my cords could be mended, but your hair? Now we were in trouble. One of your braids had gotten caught in the spokes of the front wheel as we went over the handlebars, and been chopped off. We immediately aborted the mission and went straight back to your place.

We called out soon as we came through the front door, our faces grim and tear-streaked. Your father came flying naked out of the shower, and did the preliminary medical inspections with no clothes on at all. Only when he realized there were no broken bones or stitches needed did he disappear back into the bathroom, returning with bandaids and iodine, a damp towel around his waist.

He shook his head sadly at your lopsided braid: "Just wait till your Maman gets home." Hair was a female domain; it was she that we would have to answer to for this, and we knew it. "How did you let this happen?" He was looking at me when he asked.

I slunk home, and told the story to my mother. The only thing more horrifying to me than what had happened to your hair was the sight of my very first naked man, hairy and dark and smelling of aftershave.

My mom had a logical explanation for this.

"Well, you know how the Salezes are different from us? Like how Grace lets you guys colour on the walls in Val's room, but I would kill you both if you did that here? Well, that's why Pierre had no clothes on. They're French."

This made perfect sense to me at the time.

I don't remember the day you left, I just remember you being gone. I think it was the first time I ever missed someone. Everyone else I loved never went anywhere. And France was such a far away place, farther even than Vancouver, too far away to phone, too far away to hope you would ever come back.

Twenty years later I saw your name on an ad. You had a video camera and were looking for gigs. It couldn't be you, but I called anyway.

"Is your name Valerie Salez?"

"Did you used to live in the Yukon?"

"Was your father French? Did your mother talk a lot?"

We were only blocks away. I went to your place that same night. We said the same thing to each other at exactly the same time right before you hugged me.

"You haven't changed a bit."

WALKS LIKE

THE FABRIC OF THIS MEMORY IS FADED, its edges frayed by time.

The young girl who lived it is now just a ghost inside of me. I can remember only her bones; the skin and flesh of her are brought to me in the stories of others. Mothers, uncles, and aunts remind me of the kind of child I was then.

There was the smell of Christmas everywhere, I do remember that, pine trees and woodsmoke and rumcake. The women smelled of gift perfume, the men of new sweaters.

Everywhere were voices, maybe a dozen different conversations woven together in the rise and fall of talk and laughter that is the backdrop of all my mind's snapshots of my family then, a huge room full of people connected to me by their blood.

I was sitting almost too close to the fire. Iced window panes separated us from the bitter white of winter outside. Everyone I'd ever known was still alive.

I was about four years old.

Both of my grandmothers sat in overstuffed chairs next to the fireplace, talking, a trace of Cockney, and a hint of an Irish lilt, respectively.

I sat on the thick rug between them, rolling a red metal firetruck up and down my white-stockinged legs, making motor, gear-changing, braking noises. Listening.

"You should have seen the fuss this morning, getting her into that dress, I tell you, Pat, I'd've never stood for it from any of my girls. You'd've thought I was boiling her in oil, the way she was carrying on. She wanted to wear those filthy brown corduroy pants again, imagine that, and she knows we're going to mass tonight." My mother's mother clicked her tongue and sent a stern glance in my general direction.

"That was what all my boys were like, Flo. Really, if you could have seen me the day that portrait on the wall there was taken, I swear I didn't have a nerve left for them to get on. Like pulling teeth, you know it was, to dress those four."

"Well you'd expect it from the boys, you know, it's only natural. But her, I don't understand it. Her mother always liked to dress up, and never a speck of dirt could you find on my Norah . . . look here, come here you." She curled an arthritic finger at me.

I stood up reluctantly and dragged my feet across the carpet toward her, hoping for a good spark.

"Look, see what I mean? Look at her knees, how does she do it? It's only been a couple of hours, and there's only snow on the ground out there. I couldn't find any dirt right now if I went out looking. Here, let me fix up that zipper. . . ."

My small fingers shot up to intercept her, and a rather large bolt of static electricity flashed between us. She pulled her gnarled hand back for a moment, and then brought it down on the back of mine.

"What a nasty thing to do to your poor old gran! Aren't you ashamed of yourself? Now, run and fetch us both a rum-ball, and for the love of Mary, don't get it all over the front of you."

I looked over to my other grandmother, at the shadow of an evil smile which pulled at the corners of her mouth. She winked at me, and motioned for me to be off.

"See what I mean about her, Pat? I'm worried sick she'll turn out to be an old maid. What happens when she starts school? Look, now . . . she even walks like a little boy. . . ."

"You're far too hard on her, Flo," came the voice of the mother of my father from behind me, laced with just a hint of annoyance. "She will be just fine. She just walks like that. That's just how she walks."

NO BIKINI

I HAD A SEX CHANGE ONCE, WHEN I WAS
six years old.

The Lions pool where I grew up smelled like every other
swimming pool everywhere. That's the thing about pools.
Same smell. Doesn't matter where you are.

It was summer swimming lessons, it was a little red badge
with white trim we were all after: beginners, age five to
seven. My mom had bought me a bikini.

It was one of those little girl bikinis, a two-piece, I guess
you would call it. The top part fit like a tight cut-off t-shirt,
red with blue squares on it, the bottoms were longer than
panties but shorter than shorts, blue with red squares. I had
tried it on the night before when my mom got home from
work and found that if I raised both my arms completely
above my head too quickly, the top would slide up over my flat
chest and people could see my . . . you-know-whats.

You'll have to watch out for that, my mother had stated,
her concern making lines in her forehead, *maybe I should*

have got the one-piece, but all they had was yellow and pink left. You don't like yellow either, do you?

Pink was out of the question. We had already established this.

So the blue and red two-piece it was going to have to be. I was an accomplished tomboy by this time, so I was used to hating my clothes.

It was so easy, the first time, that it didn't even feel like a crime. I just didn't wear the top part. There were lots of little boys still getting changed with their mothers, and nobody noticed me slipping out of my brown cords and striped t-shirt, and padding, bare-chested, out to the poolside alone.

Our swimming instructor was broad-shouldered and walked with her toes pointing out. She was a human bull-horn, bellowing all instructions to us and punctuating each sentence with sharp blasts on a silver whistle which hung about her bulging neck on a leather bootlace.

"Alright, beginners, everyone line up at the shallow end, boys here, girls here, come on come on come on, boys on the left, girls on the right."

It was that simple, and it only got easier after that.

I wore my trunks under my pants and changed in the boys' room after that first day. The short form of the birth name my parents bestowed me with was androgynous enough to allow my charade to proceed through the entire six weeks of swimming lessons, six weeks of boyhood, six weeks of bliss.

It was easier not to be afraid of things, like diving boards and cannonballs and backstrokes, when nobody expected you to be afraid.

It was easier to jump into the deep end when you didn't have to worry about your top sliding up over your ears. I didn't have to be ashamed of my naked nipples, because I had not covered them up in the first place.

The water running over my shoulders and back felt simple, and natural, and good.

Six weeks lasts a long time when you are six years old, so in the beginning I guess I thought the summer would never really end, that grade two was still an age away. I guess I thought that swimming lessons would continue far enough into the future that I didn't need to worry about report card day.

Or maybe I didn't think at all.

"*He* is not afraid of water over his head?" my mom read aloud in the car on the way home. My dad was driving, eyes straight ahead on the road. "*He* can tread water without a flotation device?" Her eyes were narrow, and hard, and kept trying to catch mine in the rearview mirror. "Your *son* has successfully completed *his* beginner's and intermediate badges and is ready for *his* level one?"

I stared at the toes of my sneakers and said nothing.

"Now excuse me, young lady, but would you like to explain to me just exactly what you have done here? How many people you have lied to? Have you been parading about all summer half-naked?"

How could I explain to her that it wasn't what I had done, but what I didn't do? That I hadn't lied, because no one had asked? And that I had never, not once, felt naked?

"I can't believe you. You can't be trusted with a two-piece."

I said nothing all the way home. There was nothing to say. She was right. I couldn't be trusted with a two-piece. Not then, and not now.

THREE LEFT TURNS

THE AIR SHIMMERED AND TWISTED where it met the earth. The road beneath the tires of my bike was a ribbon of dust, hard-packed and hot, a backroad race-track, and I was gaining on him.

His BMX was kicking up a cloud of pretend motorcycle smoke. I smiled and pedalled through it, teeth grinding grit and lungs burning, because the stakes were so high.

If I won, I was faster, until next time, than my Uncle Jimmy. And if he lost, he was slower, until next time, than a girl.

Is the little brother of the woman who married your father's brother related to you? I called him my Uncle Jimmy, regardless, and he was my hero.

He was four years older and almost a foot taller than me, and I don't think I ever did beat him in a bicycle race, but the threat was always there.

Just allowing a girl into the race in the first place raises the possibility that one might be beaten by a girl, so the whole situation was risky to begin with. We all knew this, and I probably wouldn't have been allowed to tag along as much as I did had I been older, or taller, or a slightly faster pedaller.

Girls complicate everything, you see, even a girl like me, who wasn't like most; you can't just pee anywhere in front of them, for instance, or let them see your bum under any circumstance, or your tears.

There were other considerations, too, precautions to be taken, rules to be observed when girls were around, some that I wasn't even privy to, because I was, after all, a girl myself.

It was the summer I turned six years old, and I was only beginning to see what trouble girls really were.

But I, it was allowed by most, *was* different, and could be trusted by Jimmy and his friends with certain classified knowledge. I was a good goalie and had my own jackknife, and could, on rare occasions, come in quite handy.

Like that day. That day I had a reason to tag along. I had been given a job to do, a job vital to the mission.

The mission was to kiss the twins. For Jimmy and his skinny friend Grant to kiss the twins.

The twins were eleven, and blonde, and from outside. Being from outside was a catch-all term used by people from the Yukon to describe people who were not from the Yukon, as in:

Well, you know how she's from outside and all, and always thought she was better than the rest of us, or, *I couldn't get the part and had to send it outside to get fixed, cost me a mint, or, well, he went outside that one winter and came back with his ear pierced, and I've wondered about him ever since.*

The twins were only there for the summer. Their dad was there to oversee the reopening of the copper mine. They wore matching everything, and also had a little sister, who was seven.

That's where I came in.

The plan was a simple man's plan, in essence. As we worked out the details, we all stood straddling our bikes in a circle at the end of Black Street where the power line cut up the side of the clay cliffs.

We were all going to pedal over to where the twins and their little sister lived. We had already hidden the supplies in the alley behind their house. The supplies consisted of a small piece of plywood and a short piece of four-by-four fence post.

We would take the plywood and prop one end of it up with the four-by-four (Jimmy and I had two uncles who were carpenters, and he would himself go on to become a plumber) and build a jump for our bikes. Then we would ride and jump off it, right in front of the twins' house, which was conveniently located right across from the park (good cover). This would enchant the unsuspecting kissees-to-be (and most likely their little sister), drawing them out from their house and into the street, where they would be easier to kiss.

We would then gallantly offer the girls a ride on the han-dlebars of our bikes, having just proven our proficiency with bike trick skills by landing any number of cool jumps. The girls would get on our handlebars, and Jimmy and Grant would ride left down the alley with the twins, and I would take a right with their little sister and keep her occupied while they carried out the rest of the mission. The kiss-the-twins mission.

The only person more likely to tell on us than the girls, after all, was their little sister, and I had it covered. Keep her occupied. Don't tell her the plan. Don't wipe out and rip the knees out of her tights. Drive her around the block a couple of times, and drop her off. Grant and Jimmy would take care of the rest.

We thought we had pretty much everything covered. We even had secondary strategies; if the jump didn't work right away, we could always make it higher, and if that didn't work, I could bravely lie on the ground right in front of it, and they could jump over me.

It was a good plan, and it worked.

What we hadn't foreseen was, I guess, unforseeable to us at the time. The girl factor, that is.

How could we have known that the twins' little sister would think that I was a boy?

And how had the girls already found out that Jimmy and Grant wanted to kiss them?

And what was I supposed to do if this girl, who was one year older than I was, slid off my handlebars as soon as we rounded the corner into the alley, planted both of her buckle-up shoes in the dust and both her hands on her hips, wanting me to kiss her like my uncle was kissing her older sister?

It hadn't crossed our minds, but that is exactly what she did (and I can't remember her name to this day, and so can't make one up, because this is a true story): the twins' little sister wanted me to kiss her, and I'm sure I must've wanted to oblige her, if only for the sake of the mission. Because that is the first most secret, sacred tomboy rule: never chicken out of the mission.

There was only one problem. The girl problem. She didn't know I was one.

It wasn't that I had deliberately misled her, it just hadn't really come up yet.

And since me kissing anyone was never part of the plan as I knew it, I had not given much thought to the girl factor. But this girl had a plan of her own.

There she was, all puckered up and expectant-like, and it seemed to me I had a full-blown situation on my six-year-old hands.

A mistake had been made, somewhere, by someone. But what was it?

I had a number of options at that point, I guess.

I could have put my left hand on the back of her yellow

dress, my right hand over her smaller left one, and given her a long, slow. . . .

No, I would have dropped my bike.

I could have leaned awkwardly over my handlebars and given her a short, sloppy one, and just hoped for the best, hoped that there wasn't something about kissing a girl the boys couldn't tell me, any slip that might reveal my true identity.

I might even have gotten away with it. Who knows? I would have liked for this story to have ended that way.

But it didn't. And because this is a true story, I would like to tell you what really went down with me and the twins' little sister in an alley by the clay cliffs the summer I turned six.

But I don't remember.

What I do recall was that unexplainable complications had arisen because we did not take the girl factor into consideration, rendering this mission impossible for me to carry out.

According to Grant and Jimmy, the little sister started to cry when the dust had cleared and she found herself alone, in an alley, in this weird little town where her dad made her come for the summer, and the twins had to take her home.

And when all three left, two weeks later, unkissed, Grant and Jimmy still considered me a major security risk.

But I don't remember my retreat.

My Aunt Norah was seventeen, and babysitting us that day. She said I came flying up the driveway, dumped my bike on her lawn, streaked past her into the living room, and threw myself on the couch, sobbing incoherently.

I would like to think that at this point she patted my head, or hugged me, or something, to calm me down, but we weren't really that kind of a family. It's not like I was bleeding or anything.

She said that when I finally calmed down enough for her to ask me what was wrong, all I could say was three words, over and over.

I don't know. I don't know. I don't know.

Girls. We can be so complicated.

STICKS AND STONES

IT SEEMED LIKE A FINE IDEA AT THE TIME. Of course, now I look back and count my ten fingers and toes, my two legs and arms that still function properly, shake my head that sits on top of the neck I have never broken, and thank my guardian angel that I still possess these blessings. But it seemed like a fine idea at the time.

My father is a welder, and his shop was located in the middle of a large and potholed industrial section just off the Alaska Highway on the edge of town. It came complete with snarling guard dogs and broken-down bulldozers, and even had its very own forgotten car and truck graveyard. If you looked up from the dusty ground and buckets of used oil, out behind colourless mechanics' shops and the skeletons of scaffolding, you could see the whole valley stretched out, the Yukon River sparkling blue and snaking through the painted postcard mountains. If you looked up, which I rarely did. There was too much to do.

There were any number of stupid and dangerous activities

to pass the day with, untold numbers of rusty edges to tear your skin and clothes on, a myriad of heavy metal objects to fall off of or get pinned beneath. I don't remember whose idea the tires were. They were not just any tires; they had once pounded dust under earth movers, or dump trucks. They were monsters, and they were everywhere. It took the whole pack of mechanics' kids and welders' daughters and crane operators' sons to move them; getting them up and onto their sides was a feat of team effort and determination, aided by crowbars we pinched from the backs of our dads' pick-ups when no one was looking. Rolling them to the edge of the power line without being noticed involved lookouts and quick action. We knew they would stop us if they found out; we didn't need to ask. The covert element of the operation only added to the thrill of it all.

Only two of us could fit in at a time, which was okay, because we had all summer and plenty of tires. Three or four kids would hold the tire steady, teetering on the edge of the cliff at the top of the power line, and two would climb inside. Kind of like gerbils on one of those exercise wheels, except you would face each other, arms and legs pushing out into the inside of the tire to hold yourself in. Gravity pretty much took care of the rest.

It was better than any roller coaster, not that any of us had been on one. It was the random element of the tire's path that did it. There was just no way to know what that tire was going to bump into or off of, and the only thing more fun than the roll down was when the tire started to come to a stop at the bottom, and did that roll-on-its-side, flip-flop dance at the bottom of the hill, kind of like a coin does when you flip it and miss and it lands on the linoleum. Only this was a huge dump truck tire with two dirty kids inside, laughing hysterically, laughing until tears ran and our sides hurt the next day. Only one of us ever puked: the heavy duty mechanic's oldest daughter lost her lunch all over her brother one day, and so we never let her ride after that, just sent her into her dad's shop to distract him while we rolled tires past his big bay doors out front.

I think it was the smell that finally gave us away. My mom kept asking me what the hell had I been up to that day while my dad was at work. There is something unmistakably foul about the smell of the inside of a tire, a cross between pond water and cat pee, I would venture, and my mom couldn't quite pin it down, but she got suspicious.

It was a bright August morning, the day it all ended, and we had a beauty of a big tire all loaded up and ready for take-off when we heard a noise inside our heads, a skull-piercing shriek that stopped our blood. We all froze in our tracks. My mom appeared from out of nowhere and it dawned on me that the noise was originating from her mouth, the words becoming slowly recognizable as she beelined toward us, her face all veins bulging red, and the whites of her eyes all you could see: "*What the fuck are you stop right now stop that stop it stop . . .*" and so forth.

There was really no explaining our way out of this one. What else could we possibly have had in mind? More damning, of course, was the pile of tires already situated at the bottom of the power line; we couldn't even argue that we were just thinking about climbing inside one and rolling it down the hill, but were just about to prudently change our minds and go help our fathers sort bolts and sweep up.

An ad-hoc committee of irate parents was called immediately, and our dads did what any fathers would have done when catching their child about to engage in activities which could only result in grievous bodily harm: they spanked us all senseless. Nothing like pain to remind you of how much you could have been hurt. It was, after all, the seventies. I was also given plenty of time to mull over my decisions for the next two weeks: I was grounded, and spent the rest of the summer inside at home, watching the Seventh Day Adventist kids safely ride their bikes on the road. What could you do? Like I said, it seemed like a fine idea at the time.

THE CAT CAME BACK

WHEN YOU'RE IRISH, AND CATHOLIC, and the oldest, you babysit a lot.

I have thirty-six cousins, so I pretty much had to book my weekends off if I had plans of my own, plans that didn't involve the baths and bedtimes of any number of little ones in pajamas, most of them with blue eyes just like mine. We all vaguely resemble each other, me and my cousins. This made it easier to get mad at them, and harder to stay that way for very long.

There was a routine, which changed only slightly, according to which aunt and/or uncle I was sitting for, which house I was in, and how many kids I had being the variables.

I would ride my bike over, or get picked up if it was winter. My uncle — no matter which one — would pull his truck up into our driveway, and honk the horn, because invariably he was late. I would skid across the ice in my running shoes, because snow boots were so uncool, and climb up into the cab of his pickup, which was usually a four-by-four, and almost always blue.

This was how things were done in my family.

This night it was my Uncle Rob behind the wheel. He was a car salesman, and always smelled like aftershave, and sometimes like rum and coke.

"Whatcha got in the backpack?" he would say.

"Homework," I would answer, usually lying.

"It's Friday night, for crying out loud," he would reply looking at me sideways, his right arm draped over the seat between us as he backed up the truck. "You read too much."

I would shrug, he would shift into first, and we'd be off.

There would be chips, and pop, and sometimes a video. There would be bathtimes, and bedtimes, and numerous glasses of water, and eventually, finally, all my cousins would be asleep.

Leaving me blissfully alone. To do whatever I liked.

This is how I discovered *Playboy* magazines, vibrators and dirty videos, condoms, feminine douches, hemorrhoid creams, and vaginal suppositories.

I have to admit that most of my earlier knowledge of the strange and smelly world of adult bodies came from snooping in the bathrooms and under the beds of my mother and father's brothers and sisters and their significant others.

Nobody had cable back then, and a girl can't keep herself occupied with CBC North all night. Boredom forced me to it, you see. My parents either had a remarkably unaccessorized sex life, or they hid things better.

Anyway, it was a Friday night that had passed like any other, and I was alone in my Uncle Rob and Aunt Cathy's bedroom. It had apparently been the scene of a rather frantic fashion crisis on his part earlier, because his clothes were strewn everywhere.

I took off my t-shirt and slipped on one of his car salesman suit jackets. It was scratchy wool on the outside, with suede sewn over the elbows. But it was lined with caramel-coloured satin inside, and felt cold and kind of nice up against my nakedness.

There was a walk-in closet, a big one, with a sliding door. Everybody had them, you know the ones, covered in mirrored tiles with gold veins running through them.

My pants didn't match, so I took them off. There was a tie, tied and then abandoned on a chairback. I slipped it over my head and slid the knot to the base of my throat. I looked left, and then right at myself, sucked my cheeks in, flexed my biceps. I tried on his cologne, slicked my hair back, and danced with myself in the mirror, singing "Jessie's Girl" by Rick Springfield.

I was a twelve-year-old dork, and I didn't care.

Except my legs looked too skinny protruding naked from his suit jacket, so I dug a pair of his clean underwear out from an open drawer and put them on. I grabbed a pair of dress socks, too, the ones made of all man-made fabrics. I believe I had every intention of putting them on my feet when I originally removed them from the drawer, but somehow they ended up down the front of the underwear. I was on my way to finding a pair of his dress pants when I was again distracted by the mirror.

I believe it was the Rolling Stones I was singing when he walked into the bedroom.

I froze, covering the bulge in my — I mean his — under-wear, and just tried to act . . . natural.

"Forgot the tickets," he said, perfectly calm, reaching for an envelope on the dresser. He stuffed the tickets into his inside pocket, turned without even cracking a smile, and was gone.

I stripped in a panic, I don't know why, having already been caught quite in the act. I couldn't believe he hadn't said anything. In my family we rarely turn down an opportunity to torture and harass each other, and he had just been handed the opportunity of a lifetime. Maybe he couldn't think of any-thing good right away, that was it, I would be in for it later, I'd never hear the end of this one, I knew it.

But he never did say a word to me about that night, not the next day, nor the next. Not even years later, both of us drunk in his boat, talking about why we both like girls, did he even ask me about it. Maybe he didn't know what to say. What do you say to your half-naked niece when you catch her in your bedroom with a pair of your dress socks stuffed down the front of a pair of your underwear, singing "Can't Get No

Satisfaction" and licking your gold-veined, mirror-tiled closet door? Maybe the shock was too much, maybe he blanked it out.

Or, maybe the black panties and fishnets I found under his and Cathy's bed weren't Cathy's, who knows?

He always was my favourite uncle.

CLOSE TO
SPIDER MAN

There are strange things done, under the midnight sun,
by the kids of the guys who work for the men who moil for gold,

The northern lights have seen queer sights,
and one of the queerest I happened to see,

took place on a night,
bathed in midnight sunlight,

A scene created and witnessed only by me.

BUT, LET ME BEGIN NEARER TO THE beginning.

I met her working the breakfast shift at the Travelodge, which was later sold and renamed the Sheffield Hotel, and then the American guy bought it and named it the Westmark, just like his hotels in Skagway, and Dawson City, and Juneau, Alaska, but, ask any of the old folks, and they still have coffee at the Travelodge, regardless of what whoever owns it now may call it.

Our shifts started at 4:30 AM to set the tables and warm up the industrial toaster, and opened for buffet and breakfast à la carte at 5:30. Busloads of retired American tourists on a last chance economical pilgrimage north to Alaska, and we were the last stop for excuse me miss, canihavesomemorecoffee?

Now, waitressing with someone can result in a very particular kind of bond, or betrayal, and only a fellow waitress can truly understand the depths of gallantry involved in pouring coffee outside of one's section, the security of a good busboy and the treachery of toast thieves, and those who don't polish their own silverware and never make coffee, and leave full buspans for the next guy.

Her name was Sylvia Wadsworth, and she was then and probably still is one of the worst waitresses I have ever apologized to hungry Texans for.

We had both just finished our first year of college. She was at Concordia, I was at Capilano College; she was going to grow up and be a psychologist, and did, and I was going to be a saxophone player with a degree, just in case my waitressing dreams fell through.

Now, a devious toast thief or lazy buspan leaver is a thing to be scorned, a thing never to pour coffee for, but a waitress who doesn't polish silverware because she is too busy cleaning blue cheese dressing out of her hair because someone left it on the top shelf of the cooler with the lid on loose is a waitress to

be rescued, in that calm, resigned yet noble way that waitresses cover for one another:

"I got the two truckers at table eight for you. They're cof-
feed and watered and their toast is on."

You do these things for one another. Especially if she's
from out of town, with a fancy name, and you're about to turn
queer that very next fall but you don't quite know it yet, all
you know is that the way the back of her neck blushes under
her tan when she accidentally pours water or coffee on American tourists makes you want to calmly, nobly, polish her silverware.

She was bilingual, and didn't have an accent when she
spoke either language, but would slip French words into her
softly-spoken English sentences in a way that made me not
care that she stole my toast:

"Je m'excuse, ma cherie, but I took your deux brun toasts.
I put more on. C'est okay, non?"

We would make fun of our customers' American accents,
and the way that wiry grey hairs grew from their noses and
ears, counting their tips and smoking and laughing conspira-
torially, as waitresses do, in the end booth, when things
slowed down.

One morning, when an unfed New Yorker was screaming at Sylvia, she backed through the double swing doors
into the kitchen, explaining in French that she actually
spoke no English at all, and so the floor manager, a five-foot

tall German closet case, approaches me:

"I'm sorry. It's about your friend. She's a sweet girl. Terrible waitress, though. One more complaint and I'm going to have to let her go. Would you talk to her for me, please?"

The way I figured it, no matter how much of her work I did for her, she only had a couple of days left to find another job.

I myself had two jobs; the other was cutting lawns for the City of Whitehorse. She asked me to see if I could get her on there, and so I did.

What she neglected to mention at the time was that she didn't know how to drive a tractor, and that she was violently allergic to grass clippings, but I helped her out a lot, and our summer not-quite-a-romance proceeded along famously.

One morning, while greasing the nipples on her tractor and talking, we discovered, small town that it was, that my mother had fired her father just a couple of months ago.

"Ta mère et mon père," she shrugged as I cleaned her air filter for her.

I got the details from my mother that night at supper.

"Jack Wadsworth? He's Sylvia's father? The man's a lunatic. Of course we had to let him go. He's a complete incompetent. Delusional. He didn't even tell his wife for two months, just kept getting up and going out like he still had a job. Sad, really. Pretended he was going to work but instead he went down to the courthouse and hung about watching the proceedings every day. Drove the bailiffs crazy. Poor Sylvia, she seems like a nice enough girl. He used to be a lawyer, they say. Sad, really, but what can you do? He's suing us, of course, representing himself. The man is a paranoid."

Sylvia's parents lived on the top floor of an old three-storey apartment building with her sister, Claudia, a mousy twenty-seven-year-old virgin in her last year of medical school, also home for the summer, working at the hospital.

One day when no one was home, Sylvia and I were out on her balcony, which was really the corner of the roof, nude sunbathing and drinking iced lattés, which I thought at the time were a French delicacy (very cosmopolitan), reading *Sassy* magazine.

My hand was touching her hand, ever so casually and accidental-like, and I think maybe I wanted to touch her but I didn't really know it yet, so luckily she interrupted my latent tendencies to read part of an article aloud to me:

"Says here that one of women's top sexual fantasies is to make love with une autre femme. Uughh. Speak for yourself, huh?"

I immediately moved my hand away from hers to sip my French latté and changed the subject.

"So . . . you wanna go swimming tomorrow?"

"I can't. I'm going white-water rafting with Greg and Jeff and all them, remember? We should put our clothes on. Mon père is going to be home from 'work' soon."

We laughed like only daughters can at their father's short-comings, and got dressed.

I heard the gory details the very next night from my best friend, Joanne.

There had been a terrible accident on the highway. Twelve teenage white-water rafters had rolled their van, Joanne's brother's girlfriend from Vancouver had been killed, cut in half in fact, going through the windshield. Sylvia had been trapped in between seats, Jaws of Life and the whole nine yards, and Sylvia's sister, the twenty-seven-year-old vir-gin/almost doctor, was driving the van because the guys were all too drunk.

But the weird part was, Sylvia's dad had shown up at the hospital, snatched both of his daughters from the emergency ward waiting room, and disappeared with them.

Police were looking for them for questioning. They hadn't received medical attention, or trauma counselling. No one was answering their phone. Joanne and I speculated at length over the drama of it all, and my mom filled in the technical details: they were driving Mr Bryant's van. Mr Bryant worked with my mom. Helped her to fire Mr Wadsworth, in fact. Mr Bryant's daughter, the gymnastics prodigy, was in the van, and was still in hospital with a leg that might not ever work right again.

And Sylvia's sister, the virgin/almost doctor, had just gotten her learner's license not days before she rolled the van.

She was relatively unhurt, but just sat at the edge of the highway afterwards, eyes staring straight ahead. She was unable to move, unable to help any of the other injured passengers.

My mom related these tragic circumstances with small-town fervor, and attention to nuance.

"This whole thing is a mess. That Jack Wadsworth better get it together and get those poor girls into hospital or they'll never recover." She tapped her temple twice with one forefinger dramatically. "Emotionally, I mean. He is deeply disturbed. It's tragic, really."

I wrote Sylvia a get well card and went by her apartment. No one answered the buzzer, so I tucked the little yellow envelope into the locked metal grate on their mailbox, and left.

When she didn't show up at work the next day, my other boss came up to me.

"So where's your little friend? She pulled a no-show on me this morning."

I hastily explained the tragic circumstances to him.

"What, she can't make a phone call? You tell her, she does it tomorrow, she's outta here."

"But her father is a lunatic," I explained patiently, because he didn't know the nuances.

"My father is a lunatic too," he returned without sympathy. "I can pick up a phone and call in."

As circumstance would have it, I mowed the lawn at the graveyard right across from her apartment building that day, and with each dusty pass on my tractor I surveyed the building for any sign of the goings-on within. Nothing all day. My little yellow get well card was still hanging forlornly out of the mailbox. As I was driving away at the end of the day my eyes shot up to the curtains: all closed. Hold on; they were all open this morning, I was sure of it, she was up there, I could feel it.

Murder-suicide? I imagined her lunatic father pacing in front of the couch, her sister sadly dead, a virgin-almost-doctor on the floor next to the china cabinet, and Sylvia, duct-taped to a chair, unable to call out the window to me as I mowed the lawn and did her share of the weed whipping.

Because people who can't waitress very well don't screw up a summer job with the city unless they're dead, or duct-taped to a chair. This was my logic.

I explained the whole fiasco to my dad that night, over a scotch. He was unenthusiastic, but unknowingly the catalyst for what was about to occur.

"If you're so fucking worried about her, quit sitting here complaining to me about it." He swirled ice cubes in his glass with a lazy turn of his wrist. "Get up off your ass, and go down there and pound on her door until someone lets you in."

He's absolutely right, I thought as I putted downtown in my Volkswagen. Do something about it.

So I snuck in through the door behind another tenant and ran up the stairs to her apartment. I could hear subdued voices behind the door, so I knocked hopefully.

The voices stopped immediately. Silence, then the sound of shuffling. But no answer.

I pounded on the door for about ten minutes, explaining that no one wanted to press charges or anything, that no one blamed Claudia; the police just wanted to talk to them, and Sylvia, you should at least call in sick or you're gonna get fired. Please open the door.

And then I heard footsteps behind the door. Finally, Jack, you've come to your senses.

But then there was a noise, just behind the door. But it wasn't a door opening kind of noise at all, it was a small, barely audible, well-oiled click of . . . well, it sounded like

The fucker's got a gun! He's behind the door, and Jesus, that sounded just like a gun!

There are times when, faced with what seems to be a life-threatening situation, that an up-until-then-ordinary person performs a feat of extraordinary bravery and/or strength, and remarkably saves the day. They later tell the reporter that they just did what anyone would have done under the circumstances, and that they really aren't a hero.

But this wasn't one of those times.

I turned and ran out the fire escape and onto the roof. But there was only another well-oiled click, and the door shut behind me, leaving me locked out, three stories up.

Needless to say, Jack didn't open this door either when I pounded, so . . . things were not really looking so good for the hero. Just me, the locked fire escape door, and an old ladder.

Of course I promptly propped the ladder up onto the roof above the locked fire escape door and climbed up. I mean, truly, what other options did I have?

I ran across the roof and dropped onto the balcony where I had almost accidentally touched her hand while sunbathing just days before; I ran without thinking, without one thought, it's true. I don't think I had one single plan in my mind at the time, but I felt so close to Spiderman that I ran right through the balcony door into the apartment of a lunatic who I thought had a gun.

I saw Sylvia, and her sister, too, still alive, for one split second before their mother pushed them both into a bedroom, and Sylvia's tear-rimmed eyes caught mine for one more second, and then she looked down, just before the door slammed shut.

Just then Jack clumsily broadsided me and I ended up on the floor, the Spiderman knocked right out of me. Then the door clicked, and I found myself alone out on the balcony again, three stories up, but with no ladder this time. I could hear Jack screaming at his wife to call the cops.

Escape would have been a fruitless endeavour, with my Spidey-senses gone, so I just paced the balcony rails, at first worrying about being gunned down out there, helpless as a hamster. Until I realized that he probably wouldn't shoot me, with the police already on their way.

This was followed by a short period of self-doubt and remorse. There was no one else to blame for my circumstance. I had acted without thought or foresight, driven by adrenaline and misguided loyalty, and here I was, with nothing to show for my valour but a carpet burn on my elbow. Not even a noble injury. I had no rescuees, no reconnaissance. I had no cigarettes.

The police sure took their time; good thing I wasn't a real burglar, and good thing he hadn't shot me, because I wouldn't have had a chance. So instead what I had was a full-on stress-related nicotine fit, and while pacing the porch, I noticed that if I peered over the railing I could see my van parked askew on the street below, my cigarettes taunting me from the dashboard.

Finally the cops arrived, and I was ushered by a freshly shorn rookie officer through the apartment and into the hallway outside their front door. I did not see Sylvia or her sister, and apparently Jack had hidden the gun. I tried to appear humble and law-abiding, because for some reason the cop was treating me like the criminal.

"So, young lady, you want to tell me just what happened here?" He rocked back on his heels, thick cop thumbs in wide cop belt.

"I sure would. This guy is a lunatic, and he's had his whole family locked up here for three days and —"

Jack interrupted me. "*She* is the lunatic, I want her charged with break and enter — she pounded on my door for twenty minutes —"

"It was only ten."

"— and when I wouldn't let her in she climbed onto the roof and broke in."

"The door wasn't even locked."

"She is a delinquent and I want her removed."

"He is a paranoid and the police are looking for him. He. . . ."

The cop silenced us both. "Well, if the police are indeed looking for him, then that is police business. We do not need you crawling around on balconies for us, do you understand me? Now I want you to go home. And don't even think about phoning or coming by here for a couple of weeks."

"A couple of weeks? He'll kill them all! They need trauma counselling, or they'll never be the same — emotionally, I mean." I tapped my temple for emphasis.

"Who?" asked the cop.

"Sylvia and her sister." Obviously he had not been briefed by his superiors.

The cop looked at Jack like they were both just humouring me. "Where are your daughters now, Mr . . . uuhh . . . Wadsworth?"

"They went to the movies several hours ago with their mother."

"He's lying!" My voice was gaining in pitch. "They're locked in the bedroom."

The cop rolled his eyes. "Don't be ridiculous. Your little friends are at the movies with their mother, and it is time for you to go. This is private property."

Apparently the police and I had different priorities when it came to serving and protecting.

When I got home, my mother was not sympathetic, either.

"You should know better than to listen to your father. What were you thinking? You could have gotten hurt. I told you that man was a lunatic. Jack Wadsworth, I mean. Your father is just obnoxious."

I never saw Sylvia again after that night. She never called in sick, quit both of her jobs, and went back to Montréal to become a psychologist. Her sister never finished her last year of medical school, and I heard that she married a helicopter logger and moved to Thunder Bay, Ontario.

So here's the epitaph: Sylvia called me once, about five years ago. She was going back up to the Yukon for Christmas, and she wondered if I was, too. She said her mom had said that I should come by for tea one day, when her father was at "work." Provided, of course, that I came through the front door this time.

We both laughed, but not like we used to. We talked a bit, and finally she asked the question.

"So . . . I gotta know, I mean, I've been wondering all of these years . . . why did you do that?"

There are certain things that cannot be explained to people who have to ask, and I guess I shouldn't have been too surprised that she didn't understand just what went down that night.

After all, she never was a very good waitress.

EGGCUPS

MY MOTHER TOLD ME ONCE NEVER TO take your eggs out of the carton and put them in the little plastic racks in the fridge door. No matter how domestic or tidy this action might seem, it is not a good idea.

"The fridge door," she said, in that knowing voice that women reserve for passing on kitchen wisdom to one another, "is slightly warmer than the rest of the fridge, and the eggs won't stay as cold there, being on the outside, and what with the door opening and closing, you are far more likely to get salmonella. Far more."

I asked what seemed the obvious thing at the time. "But then why would they keep on making fridges with little plastic egg cups in the doors then?"

My mother frowned over her glasses at me, shaking her head. "It's not a good idea," she repeated firmly.

I am a disciple, and she a prophet, bringing household revelations to the unenlightened, and this is a commandment:

Thou shalt not use thine egg cups. Not a good idea.

Of course, some years later, I made myself an egg cup omelette one night after a ten-hour work day, and spent the next three days in my tiny, bachelor's bathroom, repenting.

I used to hate it when my mother was right, but I've matured.

MANIFESTATION

I WAS WORKING IN THE YUKON AT THE time, dry-air dirt under my nails, long days in the land where the summer sun seldom sleeps. It was six o'clock in the company truck, there was sand in my teeth, and sweat left shiny trails through the dust on my face. We had planted hundreds of trees and watered them that day, and I felt sunburnt.

My work partner Kelly was a sweet-until-you-crossed-her straight girl, due in two weeks to marry my old hockey buddy, Barry Fuller, also a landscaper. His parents lived in the industrial area of town, and my uncle used to date his older sister Gale. Such is the small-town life, and its folks.

She was driving, and I turned to say something to her, but she interrupted me: "Oh my God, look at your face," she said, red-faced, stuck between a laugh and a sort of half-gasp, eyes wide.

I tilted the rear-view mirror toward the offending face and looked at my reflection.

Sweat had run down my forehead and into the lines

60

around my mouth, and perhaps I had passed a topsoiled hand over my upper lip, or maybe scratched an itchy nose with a dirty thumb, but it was a magic combination, because there it was: a dirt moustache, worn perfectly into my top lip. Sweat lines and sprinkler spray had collected a perfect line of soil there, and I had been transformed.

I looked just like a boy. To me, I looked like my long lost brother would, if I knew him. To my work partner, I looked like trouble.

"Here, here's a napkin, wipe it off, you're creeping me out. You look like my first boyfriend." She seemed a little nervous now, and would not meet my eyes.

"Is he a fag now, by any chance?" I asked, my smirk pulling up one corner of my 'stache. I winked at her. "I'm gonna leave it, it's kinda sexy, don'tcha think? I bet the girls would love it, if there were any dykes in this godforsaken land."

She shook her head and shrugged like she always did when I said anything queer, and drove.

I turned up the AM radio, and sang along to a country tune about pick-up trucks, and looked in the rear-view mirror. Couldn't help but look in the mirror. My eyes kept returning to my reflection, like a tongue to a loose tooth. Myself in a moustache. Something about it fit. It suited me, I thought.

That was the first one.

THIS, THAT, AND THE OTHER THING

I DON'T HAVE THE RECIPE WRITTEN down, so it tastes different every time. You need chipotle peppers, the smoked Mexican ones; I've seen them dried sometimes, but mostly I get the canned ones.

My friend Deanne Loubardious showed me how the first time, her striped shirtsleeves rolled up and over her tanned landscaper's forearms, and an unlit cigarette dangling in one corner of her mouth, as she chopped chicken into chunks with short, callused, dirt-worn-in fingers.

†

Step one:
First you boil the chicken in a stock pot with three or four peppers and about eight cups of water. Save the stock, let the chicken cool enough to take the bones out, and cut into bite-size pieces.

†

There is a feeling like none other that I know when I have a big batch cooling in the fridge, or simmering on the stove; it is a broad, back-turned-against-the-wolf-at-your-door kind of feeling, a you-don't-have-to-worry-about-hungry-company-showing-up-unexpected kind of feeling.

As I was about to feed my chosen family — feet planted firmly on the kitchen floor, toes staring down the dust bun-nies cowering between the stove's legs — I thought, rather stereotypically, of my mother, which is odd really, because my father is the weekend gourmet, and I cooked for my sister and me on weekdays. My mother was usually out, either working late or taking night classes; I don't have any Mrs Cleaverish memories of her in the kitchen.

But my mother knew how to cook the standards: Sunday roast with Yorkshire pudding, turkey with all the trimmings, cream of turkey on toast for leftovers, boiled-carrots kind of stuff, passed on dutifully to her by her mother, my shrinking and pale grey grandmother.

Cooking made my mother nervous; she could have made prime time commercials for boil-in-the-bag corn and Royal City canned peas. I can even see her now, exclaiming over their convenience and home-cooked goodness, snipping open bags and pulling things from a spotless microwave with red and white checkered mitts on, smiling at the camera, and truly meaning every word of it.

Holiday meals were extravagant, yet conservative, served

in heavy eighties handmade pottery bowls on matching woven placemats, cooked with great care but no love, cooked in reverence to obligation, not art.

†

Step two:

In a large, preferably cast iron pan (I'm a little old-fashioned in that way), make a roux, you know, from melted butter and flour; this will be the backbone of your cream sauce. Add a couple of cups of stock, tons of garlic, sautéed onion, and four or five more chipotles.

†

My father made Sunday breakfast for us all, crepes or waffles or buckwheat pancakes, fussed over sauces and served helpings all around with flourish and a showman's hand; he made too many dishes for what got done, ate too much, bloated, gloated over compliments from my mother's duly impressed girlfriends, and loved every last sliver of green onion of it all.

†

Step three:
While you're making the roux, boil eight or nine small

potatoes in the stock, and when they are done, strain them out and chop them into bite-size pieces. If you are like me and have yet to purchase the entire Martha Stewart pot collection, you are now going to have to pour the stock into a large bowl to cool, so that you still have a big huge pot to keep on cooking in.

†

They divorced last summer, after twenty-seven years, and my mother has lost fifty pounds since. At first, she didn't eat at all.

When I went home in August, she was a carbon copy of her former self, picking at a bagel for breakfast and drinking only hot water with a squeeze of lemon.

Someone had to teach her how to cook for one.

So I took her to the Food Fair. She pushed the cart with resignation up and down the aisles, and I circled her like a babysitter, patiently extolling the virtues of couscous and Ichiban noodles.

"Purple cabbage," I explained, "is the bachelor's very best vegetable companion. Cheap cheap, and you can leave one of these fuckers in the crisper for two months and still make coleslaw, no problem, adds colour to a salad," etc., etc.

I'm not sure where exactly I had lost her, or even if she had heard anything I'd said at all, but I looked up from the plethora of produce suddenly and realized that she wasn't listening, that in fact her eyes were focused somewhere between the wheels of the cart and the permafrost always located about three feet under the concrete foundations of anything built in the place I come from, and she had begun to cry.

"I don't care anymore, that's why. That is why I can't eat. I don't care whether I live or die." She confessed this to me, as if no one was listening, and then she shook her head, as if someone else had spoken, and she couldn't quite agree with them.

†

Step four:

Pour the sauce base and onions into the large pot, add the chicken, the potatoes, a whole whack of sliced mushrooms, zucchinis, squash maybe sometimes, carrots, and a can of chick peas (I myself never have time to soak the little fuckers). Add a few more cups of stock and stir, like a cauldron, thinking always of your mother, even if she's not Mexican and doesn't like to cook really, and simmer, adding more stock as you boil it off.

†

My mother hired a moving company when the house was sold,

and insured everything she owned. Two months before she could move into her new house on her own, the mover guy showed up, in tight Levi's and a big brass belt buckle with a front end loader on it, to drop off the boxes: special boxes, reinforced for dishes and collectibles, and long, flat boxes for pictures, and rolls and rolls of brown packing paper, tape, labels, pens, and detailed, photocopied instructions for wrapping everything.

"You have to wrap the bowls in four pieces each, four pieces, or it's not covered if anything gets broken, it says so right here. Four pieces each, or it's not covered."

She said this over and over to us all, like a mantra.

My father had conveniently left for Australia only days before, leaving her to sort, separate, itemize, wrap, box, label, or throw out everything they had collected together in the last twenty-seven years of marriage. We only moved once, six blocks down Twelfth Avenue, from Hemlock to Grove Street. My parents have had the same phone number all of my life.

I was kneeling on the carpet in the living room, packing up the cuckoo clock and an abstract stone carving of an owl, I think, listening to my mom giving orders to two of my almost uncountable cousins, Rachael and Lindsay, eleven and ten years old respectively, around the corner, in the kitchen.

"Four pieces each, remember, Rachael? Or else it's not covered, if anything gets broken."

"You throwing this out, Auntie Pat? Can I have it then?" one of them asked in her little girl falsetto.

"Lindsay," her mother, my aunt, interrupted, "what the fuck are you going to do with an hors d'oeuvres tray, you tell me? Just more junk to clutter up your room with. You can't see the floor in there as it is. Give it to the Sally Ann, Pat, it's still perfectly good," Roberta said, scrubbing the tops of the cup-boards.

"Put it wherever you want it, just get rid of it," my mom said. "I don't want to see it again. I want to get rid of most of this stuff. How we ever collected so much stuff, I don't know. I don't even remember getting some of it, much less using most of it."

Their voices faded and mixed in the back of my head, as did the sound of dishes being wrapped in brown paper, and Fleetwood Mac on the tape deck. My dad had already taken the stereo and most of the CDs, and so, ironically and down-right bittersweet at the time, we were forced to listen to sun-faded tapes from when I was a kid as we packed – I had scrubbed walls to America, vacuumed to Supertramp, sorted photos to Burton Cummings.

And now I was crying to "Lay Me Down in the Tall Grass." Tears obscured the cardboard box that I knelt in front of, and only the lump in my throat was keeping my heart from falling right out of my mouth and into the box.

I had been so busy packing and scrubbing, fending off the

inevitable and largely looming family feud, making sure my mom ate enough, and my dad didn't drink too much, that I had forgotten to mourn. Mourn the dissolution of my family, and the passing on of the only house I really remember living in.

My mom walked in to the living room and noticed the tears before I could choke them off, and dropped to her knees beside me.

"I know this is hard. It's the hardest thing I've ever done. I don't think I can make it through this. I fucked everything up, didn't I? Everything is gone, everything, and it's all my fault. This is all my fault."

Her hands meant *this*, this home packed into boxes. She held her palms up, empty.

†

Webster's *Handy Pocket College Dictionary* defines pain in the following fashion:

> *1: n. as the suffering of body or mind. 2: pl. great care (as in taking pains to ensure...). 3: v. to cause suffering to.*

Also listed is painful, an adjective.

In reference also to pain, Leslie D. Weatherhead, the author of such illuminating reads as *After Death, The Transforming Friendship, The Afterworld of the Poets, Jesus and*

Ourselves, and *The Mastery of Sex Through Psychology and Religion*, wrote in *Psychology in Service of the Soul* that with-out pain far back in the time of animal creation, we might never have come to be. We must allow a place for that minimum of pain which is how Nature warns us that something is wrong. The animal not warned by pain would have been destroyed. But there is evidence to show that when pain has given that warning, it ceases to be beneficial and becomes an evil thing.

And he cites as an example an experiment with two blis-ters inflicted by suggestion under hypnosis on a patient, one of which he suggested should be painful and the other non-painful, in which the painful one took twice as long to heal as the non-painful one. I think what he is saying is that whatev-er doesn't kill you makes you live.

Time takes the edge off of the unbearable, turns wounds into scars, agony becomes just an ache. What used to hurt all the time only bothers you when you move it just so.

Tragedy has a short shelf life.

This is how the world apologizes for being such a bitch sometimes. Eventually, crisis becomes just a circumstance, a situation that just must be dealt with.

So that's what happened. Time turned the gaping wound where my father had been into just an empty ache. Some-where between her mouth and her chest and eventually min-utes and then hours and then even days would pass between bouts of overwhelming lonely.

And this was a good thing.

†

Step five:

Right before you serve, take a cup of cooled stock and mix in five or six tablespoons of yogurt or mayonnaise, and blend until smooth. Pour this mess into the bigger mess and you have an awesome batch of spicy chipotle chicken in a light cream sauce to serve over brown rice or couscous. Make a salad, too, and you're set.

Feed yourself and three or four friends for at least three days, for about twenty-five bucks, if you have a big enough stock pot. Good for whatever ails you.

†

My mother has started to date the English chap she hired to paint her new guest bedroom. He is a creative and giving gourmet cook, and an amateur photographer. They hike a lot together.

She is taking tap dance lessons, and willow chair-making classes with a couple of girls from her office. They are all recently divorced, and just went in on a barbecue together, all having lost custody of their respective hibachis.

My father bought an airstream trailer, parked it behind

his welding shop, and has not cut back on his drinking.

I look, and cook, just like my father, but I have my mother's teeth, and tits.

THERE GOES THE BRIDE

WHAT CAN I SAY? GUESS I'LL START
with what everyone else is saying. Congratulations. So you're
all married up now. Weird, huh? Do you feel any different
than you did an hour ago? I do. That could be the three scotch-
es I had in a row, though, just to take the edge off.

Your father is freaking me out a bit. He seems rather
thrilled to see me here. He's the one pouring me drinks, he
keeps patting me on the back and saying "Good to see ya" like
I was his long lost . . . whatever. He was never this friendly
when his eldest used to sit on my face in her spare time. He
still can't remember my name, but I wouldn't hold something
like that against the guy, I always liked him, even if he is
enjoying my position in this whole affair just a little too much.

I always cry at weddings, always have. 'Member when
Laura got married in *Little House on the Prairie*? I lost it even
then. I get this from my mom.

But I was trying not to today, seemed to me the ex-lover
should remain dry-eyed, lest her feelings be misconstrued,

but the truth is even the thought of all that true love and sick-
ness and health and having and holding and all still sneaks
past my cynicism somehow and pulls at some ancient believer
in me, and I cry every time. Every time someone dares speak
such lofty hopes aloud.

He seems like a nice guy, your . . . husband. I was afraid
he'd be an asshole and I'd hate him, or that I'd be an asshole
and he'd hate me, but so far we both just smile at each other,
more like teammates than adversaries, like we both know
what it's like to step up to the plate when you're pitching.

Your friend – you know the one who never liked me so
was always extra nice? She keeps putting her hand on my arm
or my shoulder and asking, "So how *are* you?" like any minute
now I'm bound to break down and confess to her my true feelings, unleashing the bitter testament of a lonely homosexual,
but even if I were, lonely that is, I would never giver her the
pleasure. Instead I keep asking her if she has seen either of
my dates, and finally I shake her hand off me and say, "I'm
fine, for chrissakes. It's her wedding, not her funeral."

Oh, well. She was always looking for proof that I was,
indeed, an asshole. I try to be helpful.

I was just helping myself to more food – I forgot how
much food there is at these functions – and this cute little old
Irish lady struck up an interesting conversation with me:

"Couldn't help but notice how much you're enjoying my
broccoli cheese casserole there, dear."

"Did you make this?" I said. "This is some of the finest broccoli cheese casserole I've ever come across. I guess I should leave some for everybody else though, huh?"

She laughed and asked me if I played in your band, if that's where I knew you from.

"No, not exactly," I said.

"Did you work with her at the restaurant then?" she asked.

"No. No, I did not," I said.

"Down at the pub then, you work together down at the pub?"

"No, no we didn't work together down at the pub, either."

She looked puzzled, so I blurted it out. "We were lovers for a couple of years. That's how we know each other."

She didn't blink a wrinkled eye or skip a beat.

"So you take about a pound of broccoli and steam it, just a little, because you're going to bake it all for a while, once you've made your cheese sauce. You'll need some cream, not milk, and I find the older cheddar has more of a snap to it."

I laughed all the way out to the backyard, after one of your brothers rescued me and we all snuck out back to smoke a spliff.

I always liked your brothers. I see shadows of you in them sometimes, when they turn their faces just so; they feel like family, remind me of my cousins.

Your oldest brother was drunk, had his tie off already, and was feeling sentimental. "We always liked you the best, you know," he whispered, one arm slung around me, like it was a secret. "We thought you were the best of all of them."

Your little brother was stoned, self-reflective. "Ironic, eh?" he pondered. "She dumps you, to marry a guy in a kilt. Sorry, dude, no offense, but you know what I mean?"

You looked beautiful today, getting married. "She looks just radiant." Everyone kept saying it, and it's true. You did.

Your face alive with that kind of wide-eyed love that used to make even me wish that I could want that picket fence as much as you did. I could never believe like you could. We broke our hearts, you and I, figuring that one out.

But the truth is, I could never give you this. A wedding that makes your grandmother happy. What's it like? "Legiti- mate" love, I mean. The gifts and congratulations and tax relief, not to mention the relief in your father's face, what is that like?

Because I can't even imagine it, and reality provides that I probably won't ever be that blushing bride, and I don't quite cut the husband mustard, either. Motorcycles and non- monogamy, or a mortgage and a mini-van: I am old enough now to know that none of this is your fault, or even mine.

There will be no church bells for me, but I cannot bring myself to mourn the loss of something I never wanted. Toasters and linen and casserole dishes, the blessings bestowed when one does as our mothers did, I will never know, and you always had the option.

Did I mention how beautiful you look today? Happy and hopeful, what more could I wish for you? I mean, what more could I wish?

YOU'RE NOT IN KANSAS ANYMORE

IT SOUNDED LIKE SHE WAS CALLING from a pay phone, what with all the background traffic and passers-by. I had to listen to catch all the words.

"So, we have to get together to do this thing. Call me and we'll go do this thing."

We had decided to go together, for moral support. It is an intimidating task, involving forms and government agencies, unfeeling civil servants poking blank-faced into one's private self.

But it has to be done. We need to finally legally change our names. This should be easy, this should be free, but it is not.

Who came up with the plan to legally name a child the day he or she was born? Whose bright idea was that? So many mistakes to make, such a wide margin of error.

The exhausted young mother cradles her still sticky new-born to her heaving chest. She lets her head rest against the sweaty forehead of the dry-mouthed new father, and they both watch, incredulous, as this tiny life form opens and closes her still wrinkled fingers and they exclaim together:

"Let's call her Dorothy. After her grandmother."

But they have no means of foretelling young Dorothy's future. In fact, they know nothing about her at all. They only want the best for her, her parents, but she's only minutes old and they've already burdened her with a weight she will carry for years, perhaps for the rest of her life.

Because what they don't know is that Dorothy is not a Dorothy. This name will appear on birthday cards, and be felt-penned on stickers she will be forced to wear on the first day of pre-school, but it will never ring true to her ears. People will call it out and she will be obliged to come, scabby knees and baseball hat on backwards, because that is her name, and someone has called it out. But she will know that something is wrong, that someone made a tragic mistake, someone wasn't thinking straight, and now she, Dorothy, must pay for it.

Until Dorothy is old enough to stand in line at the office called Vital Statistics and name herself again.

"Her heart beat and blood pressure seem normal, doctor, it looks like the sticks and stones just missed her bones, but someone named her Dorothy. Is there anything we can do?"

Dorothy is a mechanic, one hundred and seventy-five pounds of biceps and brush-cut, and looks more like her father than her brothers do.

So, you stand in line, you fill out some forms, take out a

couple of ads in the paper, no big deal, right? You just change your name if they got it all wrong.

I'll tell you what I'm worried about: do they make you explain yourself? Does the form make you say why you feel you must change your name? State reason below. Choose one of the following. Provide documents. Use a separate sheet of unlined paper if necessary. Please print in black or blue ink only.

I can see myself, palms sweaty and stammering.

"My legal name doesn't fit the rest of me. It never has, Your Honour. See, here, how I was born with no hips at all, and how my t-shirt hides my tits? I have hair on my chest, too, and well, everyone makes mistakes. I just need one more chance to get it right, if you will just allow me to write Ivan down on this form, if it pleases the court, I would be much obliged. I just turned thirty, Your Honour, and it's time something about me matched."

This is a dramatization, of course. It probably won't be all that bad. And my name is not Dorothy.

RED SOCK
CIRCLE DANCE

August, 1974 · Whitehorse, Yukon
FIVE YEARS OLD AT THE QUANLIN MALL,
Saturday shopping, and I was holding open the swing door for
my mom and the cart. I remember I had half a cinnamon
candy stick in my mouth and a red baseball hat with the plastic thing in the back pushed through a hole that was smaller
than the smallest hole in the strap, a hole I had to make myself
with the tip of a heated bobby pin.

So the rest of the strap stuck oddly out from one side of
the back of my head, but I didn't care, because it was my
Snap-On-Tools hat that my dad had given me, just handed it
right over to me when the guy at the tool place gave it to him,
he was buying rivets or concrete pins or something, and the
hat said Northern Explosives too, in black block letters in an
arch over the hole in the back part, and come to think of it,
what I wouldn't do now for that hat.

So enough about the hat, this American tourist sees me
holding the door open, and of course he assumes it's for him,

so he won't bump his cameras together pushing past his belly to open it for himself, and he steps through the door, right in front of my mom and her groceries.

He thanks me down his nose in heavy Texan "Thank you, son," and sucks more fresh Yukon air through his teeth. He is about to speak to me again, to meet the people, to engage in a little local colour, in the form of a polite little boy, and perhaps, via a patronizing conversation with him, get to meet his lovely young mother, too, who also had my little sister in tow, perpetual snot on her upper lip, even in summer like this.

My mom interrupts this quaint northern moment, pushing the puffed wheat, two percent, and pork chop-laden cart briskly through the door. "She is not your son," she shoots out the side of her mouth and the door slams shut behind the surprised Texan. I can't see him anymore, there is just myself reflected in the dusty glass, and the back of my mom smaller in the background, as she pushed the cart and dragged my little sister to my dad's Chevy, where he was smoking behind the wheel.

We could hate the tourists a lot more back then, before the mines all shut down.

The pavement was so hot in the parking lot that the bottoms of my sneakers stuck to the tar that patched the cracks on the way back to my Dad's truck.

†

April, 1992 † Vancouver, B.C.
The van was packed when the call came.

"Is this the girl named Ivan?"

How much can you really guess about a stranger's voice on the phone, but I listened to the soft, smiling lilt of hers rise and fall as she explained that she had been at a going away party for me the night before, a surprise going away party that my friends threw for me because I was driving up to the Yukon today to work for six months. Except the surprise part of the plan had worked just a bit too well, because what nobody besides myself knew was that I was teaching twelve inmates at the Burnaby Correctional Centre for Women how to make leather belts all night, and this was the first I had heard about my own party, and it was over. Quite the surprise it was.

"Great party," she explained, and the sound of her laugh made me think of leprechauns. "Anyway, I was going to take the bus up to Whitehorse today, and well, how do you feel about some company? I cooked a whole ton of pasta salad for the bus."

Now, no amount of gas money and pasta salad can pay for four days on the Alaska Highway with someone who is starting to get on your nerves, because after Prince George you really are in the middle of nowhere, but I liked her voice. I said I'd pick her up in an hour at her sister's place on my way out of town.

Of course, driving over, the doubting began. Just me and the open road home – and a perfect stranger. What if she doesn't smoke, or wants to talk about co-dependency or something like that for two thousand miles? She'll be so glad she's not stuck on a Greyhound that she won't actually say anything; she'll just silently roll down her window in a disapproving fashion and say things like, "I should give you my therapist's number. She specializes in addiction issues."

But I picked her up, she bungee-corded her beat-up mountain bike to the roof, loaded in her pasta salad, lit a smoke, and smiled with an elf mouth that matched her leprechaun laugh as she surveyed my van and said:

"So if she breaks down, I guess I'll just double you the rest of the way on my bike."

Three nights later, in a campground somewhere just outside of Fort Nelson, she slipped her tongue into my ear and her right hand into my Levi's and whispered, "I've wanted to do this since we left Kitsilano."

Six months later, I drove back to Vancouver to go to electrical school, and she stayed. She had met a sweet-faced French-Canadian boy who I thought looked like Leif Garrett, and she was, unbeknownst to all of us at the time, pregnant with their first son.

"You gonna write me, Chris?" I asked her as we loaded the last of my stuff back into my van.

"Probably not, but I'll think about you whenever I eat

pasta salad, and if that's not love, then I've never been in it."

This is the closest thing to a commitment you will ever get from a leprechaun, and I knew this at the time.

✝

November, 1998 † Whitehorse, Yukon

It is a balmy November day at Chris' cabin, about three below zero and still no snow. The grass is frost-frozen, sparkling under a sun that shines, not cold, but heatlessly, if there is such a word.

Chris wants to get the kids together and dressed and go into town, about a half-hour drive in a four-by-four. You could still make the road right now in a car, but not after a good snowfall.

I haven't seen Frances, her middle son, since he was a babe in arms. He is now three, and his red brown curls and round face were the first thing I saw at six this morning, when I was still scotch and cigarette sandpaper-mouthed. He pulled the covers off my face and pronounced in a matter-of-fact falsetto: "I'm not sure who you are, but could you help me out?" His one hand still held the end of the sleeping bag up, and his other hand held a strip of toilet paper, which trailed across the cabin floor and into the cold storage room where I assumed he'd just performed his morning's first production.

Because Frances performs everything. He has just pranced out of his and his brother's bedroom, in a pair of emerald and blue-striped tights, red wool socks, and what looks like part of a sleeve from his dad's old orange sweater stretched up and over his chest, like a tube top.

"Dat dah da dahhh . . ." sliding in his socks on the bare floor, his smile flits and then disappears, and he comes to a full halt in front of Chris.

"Frances. Warmer clothes. It's minus three."

His shoulders drop like sandbags, and he stomps, his censored artist head down, back to wardrobe, to change. Thirty seconds later, sliding socks and all, he is back out for act two, but with a purple hippie scarf he is whirling around his neck and twirling . . . his red socks making circles and figure eights, he knows no fear of slivers. . . .

"A sweater. For chrissakes, Frances, don't you want to go into town with Ivan?"

Again with the shoulders, and eventually he is forced to compromise his ensemble altogether and submit to a sweater, and a toque as well. I know how he feels — nobody wears a toque and a tube top at the same time, and then to have to cover it all with a sweater?

"What do you think of my three-year-old drag queen, Ivan?" Chris asks me like she is showing me a brand new old car she just bought with her own money. She thinks that he will be my favourite because he is . . . well, just like me, and

I always thought it would be Emile, because he was the first, and because I was inside of her when he was in her belly and when she came I felt him kick and knew the magic of him then. And then there was Gailon, too, and my mom said Chris told her in the truck one day that it was too late for an abortion with him, and that Chris cried when the midwife handed her her third boy, that makes four boys now and her, alone in the cabin, and she knew Gailon was going to be the last of it.

But Chris never told me any of this, she just told my mom, and now Gailon sits, too, under his crown of cotton ball hair and watches me eat an egg and toast. He is one-and-a-half and drinks cranberry tea from a mug with the rest of us. The kids picked the cranberries themselves.

Gailon looks like a little old man shrunk right down, like an owl. There is no baby in his face, and my mom says he will be the most special because Chris almost didn't have him, so he is more of a gift that way. But all Chris tells me is that she has been breast-feeding for five years now, and I couldn't see her in the dark last night when we touched, but her hands felt older.

She smells of wood smoke, and I smell of hair products, and everytime I see her the boys are bigger and there is somehow less of her and I meet her sons again, three secrets of her unfolding into their own in a tiny cabin forty miles from anything.

No wonder Chris couldn't wait for me and Frances to meet again. Now that he's walking and talking, and putting on shows. Now that we can relate as equals, he and I. Sure, he's only three, but age has never mattered to a true queen, and it takes one to know one.

Say what you will of nature and nurture and the children of both, scientists and sociologists and endocrinologists and psychologists and psychiatrists and therapists and plastic surgeons can all have their theories, but none of them can explain to me this:

How did Frances get to be Frances in all his Francesness? He doesn't watch TV. He listens to CBC. Frances doesn't know that boys don't wear tube tops. No one has told him this. He just has to wear a sweater too, if it's winter. The magic of this is not lost on me.

He doesn't get it from his father, who doesn't eat anything he doesn't grow, or pick, or preferably shoot, skin, and dress himself with, and his older brother is a five-year-old water-packing, bicepped bushman in his own right, and Gailon is only a year and a half.

All four boys seem well aware that Chris is the only female in the house; she owns the only two breasts, the only one without what they have.

Yet Frances, three years old, triumphs like a crocus in a crack in a cliff; how does a lonesome queen even know he exists in a cabin in a frozen field in the Yukon with apparently not another soul around, with an ounce of fashion sense, or even the most minute grasp of the immense and innate drama of it all for miles?

No one but Frances. Until mom drags Uncle Ivan home for a night or two.

This is why I must be there for him, for all those moments, for those drag queen equivalents of baptism, first communion, confirmation, priest, and sainthood, and so on.

The first time he finds the right outfit, the one that really fits, I will hold up the mirror for him and say, "You go, girl." If he wants his ears pierced, he can count on me. The first time he gives the captain of the basketball team a secret blowjob, I will be his confessor. The first time someone calls him a faggot, and he slowly comes to realize that they don't think a faggot is a good thing to be at all, the first time he feels that fear, I want to be there. I will tell him of the time he was three and first did the red sock circle dance in the orange tube top ensemble. I will tell him then that he was born a special kind of creature, one that God never meant for everyone to understand, but that I understand. I will tell him that I will always love that little flower of him, that perfect unknowing differentness that blossomed and danced in a frozen field in spite of everything.

Because drag queens always dance in spite of everything. It's part of the job description.

How can I look at him and not feel relief? He is living proof that I was just born this way. I don't remember my version of the red sock circle dance, but ten to one someone told me to close my legs because you could see my panties when I danced like that, and how do you spell *unladylike*?

But things will be different for Frances, he who will start kindergarten in the year 2000.

Chris and I load the boys into the truck and head into town. I am on a mission: I am taking Frances to meet more of his people.

My friend Cody, the legendary creature with painted nails and black ringlets that reach halfway down his back. It is rumoured that he is a hermaphrodite, that he possesses extra plumbing, perhaps special powers. I have never asked him, because it is none of my business, and Cody has never inquired about the bulge in my own pants. He is a creature of immense grace and beauty, and that is all I need to know.

I take Frances into the cafe where Cody works, to introduce them to each other with all the pomp and circumstance required when in the presence of royalty.

"Cody, I'd like you to meet my godson, Frances. Frances, this is Cody."

But Frances doesn't acknowledge Cody, or his ringlets, or his fingernails at all. Something else more pressing has caught his attention. He reaches his small hand up to caress the fabric of Cody's silver velvet shirt, tight and shimmering over his slender torso. Frances smiles in wonder to himself and his mother places her hand on my shoulder, and laughs like a leprechaun.

"That's my boy," she says, and for a second I am unsure whether she is referring to Frances, Cody, or myself, but it doesn't matter, because we are all where we belong. Home.

photo: jamie griffiths

Ivan E. Coyote is a writer and circus performer, and a
member of the celebrated performance collective Taste This,
who collaborated on *Boys Like Her* (Press Gang, 1998),
a critically acclaimed and award-winning book on
gender and desire. Ivan lives in Vancouver.